Musical Chairs and Dancing Bears

Joanne Rocklin • pictures by Laure de Matharel

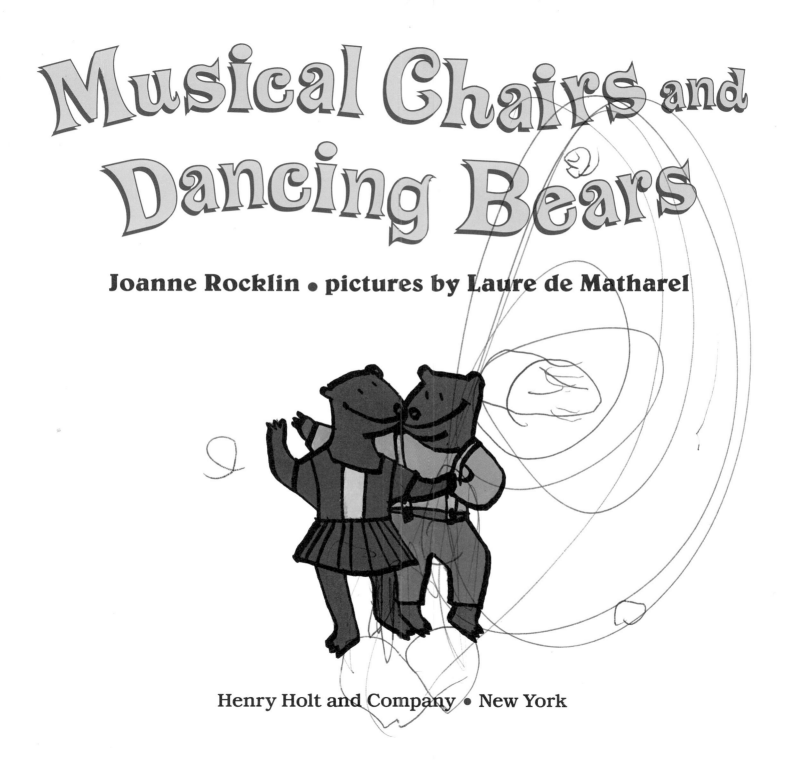

Henry Holt and Company • New York

For Nancy Smiler Levinson, a true friend indeed
—J. R.

For Claire
—L. de M.

Published by Henry Holt and Company, Inc.,
115 West 18th Street, New York, New York 10011.
Published simultaneously in Canada by Fitzhenry & Whiteside Ltd.,
91 Granton Drive, Richmond Hill, Ontario L4B 2N5.
First edition

Library of Congress Cataloging-in-Publication Data
Rocklin, Joanne.
Musical chairs and dancing bears / Joanne Rocklin; illustrated by
Laure de Matharel.
Summary: Bears demonstrate simple subtraction and a variety of
dances and musical rhythms while playing musical chairs.
ISBN 0-8050-2374-7 (alk. paper)
[1. Games—Fiction. 2. Bears—Fiction. 3. Dancing—Fiction.
4. Counting. 5. Stories in rhyme.] I. De Matharel, Laure, ill. II. Title.
PZ8.3.R595Mu 1993   [E]—dc20   92-41078

Printed in the United States of America
on acid-free paper. ∞

1 3 5 7 9 10 8 6 4 2

Let's play!

Ten dancing bears
Only nine chairs—

Waltz!
DUM-dee-dee
DUM-dee-dee
DUM-dee-dee
DUM—

Nine dancing bears
Only eight chairs—

Rock!
Groovin' and movin' and
Clappin' and snappin' and
Whirlin' and twirlin' and—

Eight dancing bears
Only seven chairs––

Square dance!
Swing your partner
Do-si-do
Promenade right
And away we go!—

Seven dancing bears
Only six chairs—

Bunny hop!
DA-da DA-da DA DA
DA-da DA-da DA
DA-da DA-da DA DA
Hop hop hop!—

Six dancing bears
Only five chairs—

Polka!
UMP-pah-pah
UMP-pah-pah
UMP-pah-pah
UMP—

Five dancing bears
Only four chairs—

Tap!
STAMP hop-shuffle-step
tap-TAP tap-TAP—

Four dancing bears
Only three chairs—

Tango!
SLIDE boom boom boom
Bar-OOM-boom boom boom
GLIDE boom boom boom
Bar-OOM-boom boom boom—

Three dancing bears
Only two chairs—

Russian kazachok!
YUM pum pum pum
Yada-lada pum pum
YUM pum pum pum
Yada-lada HEY!—

Two dancing bears
Only one chair—

Ballet!
Jeté, plié
Pirouette
Jeté, plié, passé—

One dancing bear
No more chairs!

BRAVO! BRAVO!

Let's play again!
Ten dancing bears....